THE STARCOMBER

Positronic Publishing
PO Box 632
Floyd VA 24091

ISBN 13: 978-1-62755-087-1

First Positronic Publishing Edition
10 9 8 7 6 5 4 3 2 1

THE STARCOMBER

ALFRED BESTER

Take two parts of Beelzebub, two of Israfel, one of Monte Cristo, one of Cyrano, mix violently, season with mystery and you have Mr. Solon Aquila. He is tall, gaunt, sprightly in manner, bitter in expression, and when he laughs his dark eyes turn into wounds. His occupation is unknown. He is wealthy without visible means of support. He is seen everywhere and understood nowhere. There is something odd about his life.

This is what's odd about Mr. Aquila, and you can make what you will of it. When he walks he is never forced to wait on a traffic signal. When he desires to ride there is always a vacant taxi on hand. When he bustles into his hotel an elevator always happens to be waiting. When he enters a store, a salesclerk is always free to serve him. There always happens to be a table available for Mr. Aquila in restaurants. There are always last-minute ticket returns when he craves entertainment at sold-out shows.

You can question waiters, hack drivers, elevator girls, salesmen, box-office men. There is no conspiracy. Mr. Aquila does not bribe or blackmail for these petty conveniences. In any case, it would not be possible for him to bribe or blackmail the automatic clock that governs the city traffic signal system. These things, which make life so convenient for him, simply happen. Mr. Solon Aquila is never disappointed. Presently we shall hear about his first disappointment and see what it led to.

Mr. Aquila has been seen fraternizing in low saloons, in middle saloons, in high saloons. He has been met in bagnios, at coronations, executions, circuses, magistrate's courts and handbook offices. He has been known to buy antique cars, historic jewels, incunabula, pornography, chemicals, porro prisms, polo ponies and full-choke shotguns.

"HmimelHerrGottSeiDank! I'm crazy, man, crazy. Eclectic, by God," he told a flabbergasted department store president. "The Weltmann type, nicht wahr? My ideal: Goethe. Tout le monde. God damn."

He spoke a spectacular tongue of mixed metaphors and meanings. Dozens of languages and dialects came out in machine-gun bursts. Apparently he also lied *ad libitum*.

"Sacré bleu. Jeez!" he was heard to say once. "Aquila from the Latin. Means aquiline. O tempora O mores. Speech by Cicero. My ancestor."

And another time: "My idol: Kipling. Took my name from him. Aquila, one of his heroes. God damn. Greatest Negro writer since *Uncle Tom's Cabin*."

On the morning that Mr. Solon Aquila was stunned by his first disappointment, he bustled into the atelier of Lagan & Derelict, dealers in paintings, sculpture and rare objects of art. It was his intention to buy a painting. Mr. James Derelict knew Aquila as a client. Aquila had already purchased a Frederic Remington and a Winslow Homer some time ago when, by another odd coincidence, he had bounced into the Madison Avenue shop one minute after the coveted paintings went up for sale. Mr. Derelict had also seen Mr. Aquila boat a prize striper at Montauk.

"Bon soir, bel esprit, God damn, Jimmy," Mr. Aquila said. He was on first name terms with everyone. "Here's a cool day for color, oui! Cool. Slang. I have in me to buy a picture."

"Good morning, Mr. Aquila," Derelict answered. He had the seamed face of a cardsharp, but his blue eyes were honest and his smile was disarming. However at this moment his smile seemed strained, as though the volatile appearance of Aquila had unnerved him.

"I'm in the mood for your man, by Jeez," Aquila said, rapidly opening cases, fingering ivories and tasting the porcelains. "What's his name, my old? Artist like Bosch. Like Heinrich Kley. You handle him, parbleu, exclusive. O si sic omnia, by Zeus!"

"Jeffrey Halsyon?" Derelict asked timidly.

"Oeil de boeuf!" Aquila cried. "What a memory. Chryselephantine. Exactly the artist I want. He is my favorite. A monochrome, preferably. A small Jeffrey Halsyon for Aquila, bitte. Wrap her up."

"I wouldn't have believed it," Derelict muttered.

"Ah! Ah-ha? This is not 100 proof guaranteed Ming," Mr. Aquila exclaimed brandishing an exquisite vase. "Caveat emptor, by damn. Well, Jimmy? I snap my fingers. No Halsyons in stock, old faithful?"

"It's extremely odd, Mr. Aquila," Derelict seemed to struggle with himself. "Your coming in like this. A Halsyon monochrome arrived not five minutes ago."

"You see? Tempo ist Richtung. Well?"

"I'd rather not show it to you. For personal reasons, Mr. Aquila."

"HimmelHerrGott! Pourquoi? She's bespoke?"

"N-no, sir. Not for *my* personal reasons. For your personal reasons."

"Oh? God damn. Explain myself to me."

"Anyway, it isn't for sale, Mr. Aquila. It can't be sold."

"For why not? Speak, old fish and chips."

"I can't say, Mr. Aquila."

"Zut alors! Must I judo your arm, Jimmy? You can't show. You can't sell. Me, internally, I have pressurized myself for a Jeffrey Halsyon. My favorite. God damn. Show me the Halsyon or sic transit gloria mundi. You hear me, Jimmy?"

Derelict hesitated, then shrugged. "Very well, Mr. Aquila. I'll show you."

Derelict led Aquila past cases of china and silver, past lacquer and bronzes and suits of shimmering armor to the gallery in the rear of the shop where dozens of paintings hung on the gray velour walls, glowing under warm spotlights. He opened a drawer in a Goddard breakfront and took out an envelope. On the envelope was printed BABYLON INSTITUTE. From the envelope Derelict withdrew a dollar bill and handed it to Mr. Aquila.

"Jeffrey Halsyon's latest," he said.

With a fine pen and carbon ink, a cunning hand had drawn another portrait over the face of George Washington on the dollar bill. It was a hateful, diabolic face set in a hellish background. It was a face to strike terror, in a scene to inspire loathing. The face was a portrait of Mr. Aquila.

"God damn," Mr. Aquila said.

"You see, sir? I didn't want to hurt your feelings."

"Now I must own him, big boy." Mr. Aquila appeared to be fascinated by the portrait. "Is she accident or for purpose? Does Halsyon know myself? Ergo sum."

"Not to my knowledge, Mr. Aquila. But in any event I can't sell the drawing. It's evidence of a felony . . . mutilating United States currency. It must be destroyed."

"Never!" Mr. Aquila returned the drawing as though he feared the dealer would instantly set fire to it. "Never, Jimmy. Nevermore quoth the raven. God damn. Why does he draw on money, Halsyon? My picture, pfui. Criminal libels but n'importe. But pictures on money? Wasteful. Joci causa."

"He's insane, Mr. Aquila."

"No! Yes? Insane?" Aquila was shocked.

"Quite insane, sir. It's very sad. They've had to put him away. He spends his time drawing these pictures on money."

"God damn, mon ami. Who gives him money?"

"I do, Mr. Aquila; and his friends. Whenever we visit him he begs for money for his drawings."

"Le jour viendra, by Jeez! Why you don't give him paper for drawings, eh, my ancient of days?"

Derelict smiled sadly. "We tried that, sir. When we gave Jeff paper, he drew pictures of money."

"HimmelHerrGott! My favorite artist. In the looney bin. Eh bien. How in the holy hell am I to buy paintings from same if such be the case?"

"You won't, Mr. Aquila. I'm afraid no one will ever buy a Halsyon again. He's quite hopeless."

"Why does he jump his tracks, Jimmy?"

"They say it's a withdrawal, Mr. Aquila. His success did it to him."

"Ah? Q.E.D. me, big boy, Translate."

"Well, sir, he's still a young man; in his thirties and very immature. When he became so very successful, he wasn't ready for it. He wasn't prepared for the responsibilities of his life and his career. That's what the doctors told me. So he turned his back on everything and withdrew into childhood."

"Ah? And the drawing on money?"

"They say that's his symbol of his return to childhood, Mr. Aquila. It proves he's too young to know what money is for."

"Ah? Oui. Ja. Astute, by crackey. And my portrait?"

"I can't explain that, Mr. Aquila, unless you have met him in the past and he remembers you somehow. Or it may be a coincidence."

"Hmmm. Perhaps. So. You know something, my attic of Greece? I am disappointed. Je n'oublierai jamais. I am most severely disappointed. God damn. No more Halsyons ever? Merde. My slogan. We must do something about Jeffrey Halsyon. I will not be disappointed. We must do something."

Mr. Solon Aquila nodded his head emphatically, took out a cigarette, took out a lighter, then paused, deep in thought. After a long moment, he nodded again, this time with decision, and did an astonishing thing. He returned the lighter to his pocket, took out another, glanced around quickly and lit it under Mr. Derelict's nose.

Mr. Derelict appeared not to notice. Mr. Derelict appeared, in one instant, to be frozen. Allowing the lighter to burn, Mr. Aquila placed it carefully on a ledge in front of the art dealer who stood before it without moving. The orange flame gleamed on his glassy eyeballs.

Aquila darted out into the shop, searched and found a rare Chinese crystal globe. He took it from its case, warmed it against his heart and peered into it. He mumbled. He nodded. He returned the globe to the case, went to the cashier's desk, took a pad and pencil and began ciphering in symbols that bore no relationship to any language or any graphology. He nodded again, tore up the sheet of paper and took out his wallet.

From the wallet he removed a dollar bill. He placed the bill on the glass counter, took an assortment of fountain pens from his vest pocket, selected one and unscrewed it. Carefully shielding his eyes, he allowed one drop to fall from the pen point onto the bill. There was a blinding flash of light. There was a humming vibration that slowly died.

Mr. Aquila returned the pens to his pocket, carefully picked up the bill by a corner and ran back into the picture gallery where the art dealer still stood staring glassily at the orange flame. Aquila fluttered the bill before the sightless eyes.

"Listen, my ancient," Aquila whispered. "You will visit Jeffrey Halsyon this afternoon. N'est-ce pas? You will give him this very own coin of the realm when he asks for drawing materials. Eh? God damn." He removed

Mr. Derelict's wallet from his pocket, placed the bill inside and returned the wallet.

"And this is why you make the visit," Aquila continued. "It is because you have had an inspiration from le Diable Boiteux. Nolens volens, the lame devil has inspired you with a plan for healing Jeffrey Halsyon. God damn. You will show him samples of his great art of the past to bring him to his senses. Memory is the all-mother. HimmelHerrGott. You hear me, big boy? You do what I say. Go today and devil take the hindmost."

Mr. Aquila picked up the burning lighter, lit his cigarette and permitted the flame to go out. As he did so, he said: "No, my holy of holies! Jeffrey Halsyon is too great an artist to languish in durance vile. He must be returned to this world. He must be returned to me. È sempre l'ora. I will not be disappointed. You hear me, Jimmy? I will not!"

"Perhaps there's hope, Mr. Aquila," James Derelict said. "Something's just occurred to me while you were talking . . . a way to bring Jeff back to sanity. I'm going to try it this afternoon."

*

As he drew the face of the Faraway Fiend over George Washington's portrait on a bill, Jeffrey Halsyon dictated his autobiography to nobody.

"Like Cellini," he recited. "Line and literature simultaneously. Hand in hand, although all art is one art, holy brothers in barbiturate, near ones and dear ones in nembutal. Very well. I commence: I was born. I am dead. Baby wants a dollar. No—"

He arose from the padded floor and raged from padded wall to padded wall, envisioning anger as a deep purple fury running into the pale lavenders of recrimination by the magic of his brushwork, his chiaroscuro, by the clever blending of oil, pigment, light and the stolen genius of Jeffrey Halsyon tom from him by the Faraway Fiend whose hideous face—

"Begin anew," he muttered. "We darken the highlights. Start with the under-painting . . ." He squatted on the floor again, picked up the quill drawing pen whose point was warranted harmless, dipped it into carbon ink whose contents were warranted poisonless, and applied himself to the monstrous face of the Faraway Fiend which was replacing the first President on the dollar.

"I was born," he dictated to space while his cunning hand wrought beauty and horror on the banknote paper. "I had peace. I had hope. I had art. I had peace. Mama. Papa. Kin I have a glass of water? Oooo! There was a big bad bogey man who gave me a bad look; and now baby's afraid. Mama! Baby wantsa make pretty pictures onna pretty paper for Mama and Papa. Look, Mama. Baby makin' a picture of the bad bogey man with a mean look, a black look with his black eyes like pools of hell, like cold fires of terror, like faraway fiends from faraway fears— Who's that!"

The cell door unbolted. Halsyon leaped into a corner and cowered, naked and squalling, as the door was opened for the Faraway Fiend to enter. But it was only the medicine man in his white jacket and a stranger man in black suit, black homburg, carrying a black portfolio with the initials J. D. lettered on it in a bastard gold Gothic with lubricous overtones of Goudy and Baskerville.

"Well, Jeffrey?" the medicine man inquired heartily.

"Dollar?" Halsyon whined. "Kin baby have a dollar?"

"I've brought an old friend, Jeffrey. You remember Mr. Derelict?"

"Dollar," Halsyon whined. "Baby wants a dollar."

"What happened to the last one, Jeffrey? You haven't finished it yet, have you?"

Halsyon sat on the bill to conceal it, but the medicine man was too quick for him. He snatched it up and he and the stranger-man examined it.

"As great as all the rest," Derelict sighed. "Greater! What a magnificent talent wasting away. . . ."

Halsyon began to weep. "Baby wants a dollar!" he cried.

The stranger man took out his wallet, selected a dollar bill and handed it to Halsyon. As soon as Halsyon touched it, he heard it sing and he tried to sing with it, but it was singing him a private song so he had to listen.

It was a lovely dollar; smooth but not too new, with a faintly matte surface that would take ink like kisses. George Washington looked reproachful but resigned, as though he was used to the treatment in store for him. And indeed he might well be, for he was much older on this dollar. Much older than on any other for his serial number was 5,271,009 which made him 5,000,000 years old and more, and the oldest he had ever been before was 2,000,000.

As Halsyon squatted contentedly on the floor and dipped his pen in the ink as the dollar told him to, he heard the medicine man say, "I don't think I should leave you alone with him, Mr. Derelict."

"No, we must be alone together, doctor. Jeff always was shy about his work. He could only discuss it with me privately."

"How much time would you need?"

"Give me an hour."

"I doubt very much whether it'll do any good."

"But there's no harm trying?"

"I suppose not. All right, Mr. Derelict. Call the nurse when you're through."

The door opened; the door closed. The stranger-man named Derelict put his hand on Halsyon's shoulder in a friendly, intimate way. Halsyon looked up at him and grinned cleverly, meanwhile waiting for the sound of the bolt in the door. It came; like a shot, like a final nail in a coffin.

"Jeff, I've brought some of your old work with me," Derelict said in a voice that was only approximately casual. "I thought you might like to look it over with me."

"Have you got a watch on you?" Halsyon asked.

Restraining his start of surprise at Halsyon's normal tone, the art dealer took out his pocket watch and displayed it.

"Lend it to me for a minute."

Derelict unchained the watch and handed it over. Halsyon took it carefully and said, "All right. Go ahead with the pictures."

"Jeff!" Derelict exclaimed. "This is you again, isn't it? This is the way you always—"

"Thirty," Halsyon interrupted. "Thirty-five, forty, forty-five, fifty, fifty-five, ONE." He concentrated on the flicking second hand with rapt expectation.

"No, I guess it isn't," the dealer muttered. "I only imagined you sounded—Oh well." He opened the portfolio and began sorting mounted drawings.

"Forty, forty-five, fifty, fifty-five, TWO."

"Here's one of your earliest, Jeff. Remember when you came into the gallery with the roughs and we thought you were the new polisher from the agency? Took you months to forgive us. You always claimed we bought your first picture just to apologize. Do you still think so?"

"Forty, forty-five, fifty, fifty-five, THREE."

"Here's that tempera that gave you so many heartaches. I was wondering if you'd care to try another? I really don't think tempera is as inflexible as you claim and I'd be interested to have you try again now that your technique's so much more matured. What do you say?"

"Forty, forty-five, fifty, fifty-five, FOUR."

"Jeff, put down that watch."

"Ten, fifteen, twenty, twenty-five . . ."

"What the devil's the point of counting minutes?"

"Well," Halsyon said reasonably, "sometimes they lock the door and go away. Other times they lock up and stay and spy on you. But they never spy longer than three minutes so I'm giving them five just to make sure. FIVE."

Halsyon gripped the pocket watch in his big fist and drove the fist cleanly into Derelict's jaw. The dealer dropped without a sound. Halsyon dragged him to the wall, stripped him naked, dressed himself in his clothes, repacked the portfolio and closed it. He picked up the dollar bill and pocketed it. He picked up the bottle of carbon ink warranted nonpoisonous and smeared the contents over his face.

Choking and shouting, he brought the nurse to the door.

"Let me out of here," Halsyon cried in a muffled voice. "That maniac tried to drown me. Threw ink in my face. I want out!"

The door was unbolted and opened. Halsyon shoved past the nurse-man, cunningly mopping his blackened face with a hand that only masked it more. As the nurse-man started to enter the cell, Halsyon said, "Never mind Halsyon. He's all right. Get me a towel or something. Hurry!"

The nurse-man locked the door again, turned and ran down the corridor. Halsyon waited until he disappeared into a supply room, then turned and ran in the opposite direction. He went through the heavy doors to the main wing corridor, still cleverly mopping, still sputtering with cunning indignation. He reached the main building. He was halfway out and still no alarm. He knew those brazen bells. They tested them every Wednesday noon.

It's like a game, he told himself. It's fun. It's nothing to be scared of. It's being safely, sanely, joyously a kid again and when we quit playing, I'm going home to mama and dinner and papa reading me the funnies and I'm a kid again, really a kid again, forever.

There still was no hue and cry when he reached the main floor. He complained about his indignity to the receptionist. He complained to the protection guards as he forged James Derelict's name in the visitors' book, and his inky hand smeared such a mess on the page that the forgery was undetected. The guard buzzed the final gate open. Halsyon passed through into the street, and as he started away he heard the brass of the bells begin a clattering that terrified him.

He ran. He stopped. He tried to stroll. He could not. He lurched down the street until he heard the guards shouting. He darted around a comer, and another, tore up endless streets, heard cars behind him, sirens, bells, shouts, commands. It was a ghastly Catherine Wheel of flight. Searching desperately for a hiding place, Halsyon darted into the hallway of a desolate tenement.

Halsyon began to climb the stairs. He went up three at a clip, then two, then struggled step by step as his strength failed and panic paralyzed him. He stumbled at a landing and fell against a door. The door opened. The Faraway Fiend stood within, smiling briskly, rubbing his hands.

"Glückliche Reise," he said. "On the dot. God damn. You twenty-three skidooed, eh? Enter, my old. I'm expecting you. Be it never so humble . . ."

Halsyon screamed.

"No, no, no! No Sturm und Drang, my beauty," Mr. Aquila clapped a hand over Halsyon's mouth, heaved him up, dragged him through the doorway and slammed the door.

"Presto-changeo," he laughed. "Exit Jeffrey Halsyon from mortal ken. Dieu vous garde."

Halsyon freed his mouth, screamed again and fought hysterically, biting and kicking. Mr. Aquila made a clucking noise, dipped into his pocket and brought out a package of cigarettes. He flipped one out of the pack expertly and broke it under Halsyon's nose. The artist at once subsided and suffered himself to be led to a couch, where Aquila cleansed the ink from his face and hands.

"Better, eh?" Mr. Aquila chuckled. "Non habit-forming. God damn. Drinks now called for."

He filled a shot glass from a decanter, added a tiny cube of purple ice from a fuming bucket, and placed the drink in Halsyon's hand. Compelled by a gesture from Aquila, the artist drank it off. It made his brain buzz. He stared around, breathing heavily. He was in what appeared to be the luxurious waiting room of a Park Avenue physician. Queen Anne furniture. Axminster rug. Two Hogarths and a Copley on the wall in gilt frames. They were genuine, Halsyon realized with amazement. Then, with even more amazement, he realized that he was thinking with coherence, with continuity. His mind was quite clear.

He passed a heavy hand over his forehead. "What's happened?" he asked faintly. "There's like . . . Something like a fever behind me. Nightmares."

"You have been sick," Aquila replied. "I am blunt, my old. This is a temporary return to sanity. It is no feat, God damn. Any doctor can do it. Niacin plus carbon dioxide. Id genus omne. Only temporary. We must search for something more permanent."

"What's this place?"

"Here? My office. Anteroom without. Consultation room within. Laboratory to left. In God we trust."

"I know you," Halsyon mumbled. "I know you from somewhere. I know your face."

"Oui. You have drawn and redrawn me in your fever. Ecce homo. But you have the advantage, Halsyon. Where have we met? I ask myself." Aquila put on a brilliant speculum, tilted it over his left eye and let it shine into Halsyon's face. "Now I ask you. Where have we met?" Hypnotized by the fight, Halsyon answered dreamily. "At the Beaux Arts Ball . . . A long time ago. . . . Before the fever . . ."

"Ah? Si. It was one half year ago. I was there. An unfortunate night."

"No. A glorious night . . . Gay, happy fun . . . Like a school dance . . . Like a prom in costume . . .

"Always back to the childhood, eh?" Mr. Aquila murmured. "We must attend to that. Cetera desunt, young Lochinvar. Continue."

"I was with Judy. . . . We realized we were in love that night. We realized how wonderful life was going to be. And then you passed and looked at me. . . . Just once. You looked at me. It was horrible."

"Tch!" Mr. Aquila clicked his tongue in vexation. "Now I remember said incident. I was unguarded. Bad news from home. A pox on both my houses."

"You passed in red and black. . . . Satanic. Wearing no mask. You looked at me . . . A red and black look I never forgot. A look from black eyes like pools of hell, like cold fires of terror. And with that look you robbed me of everything . . . of joy, of hope, of love, of life. . . ."

"No, no!" Mr. Aquila said sharply. "Let us understand ourselves. My carelessness was the key that unlocked the door. But you fell into a chasm of your own making. Nevertheless, old beer and skittles, we must alter same." He removed the speculum and shook his finger at Halsyon. "We must bring you back to the land of the living. Auxilium ab alto. Jeez. That is for why I have arranged this meeting. What I have done I will undone, eh? But you must climb out of your own chasm. Knit up the raveled sleeve of care. Come inside."

He took Halsyon's arm, led him down a paneled hall, past a neat office and into a spanking white laboratory. It was all tile and glass with shelves of reagent bottles, porcelain filters, an electric oven, stock jars of acids, bins of raw materials. There was a small round elevation in the center of the floor, a sort of dais. Mr. Aquila placed a stool on the dais, placed Halsyon on the stool, got into a white lab coat and began to assemble apparatus.

"You," he chatted, "are an artist of the utmost. I do not dorer la pilule. When Jimmy Derelict told me you were no longer at work, God damn! We must return him to his muttons, I said. Solon Aquila must own many canvases of Jeffrey Halsyon. We shall cure him. Hoc age."

"You're a doctor?" Halsyon asked.

"No. Let us say, a warlock. Strictly speaking a witch-pathologist. Very high class. No nostrums. Strictly modern magic. Black magic and white magic are passé, n'est-ce pas? I cover entire spectrum, specializing mostly in the 15,000 angstrom band."

"You're a witch-doctor? Never!"

"Oh yes."

"In this kind of place?"

"Ah-ha? You too are deceived, eh? It is our camouflage. Many a modem laboratory you think concerns itself with tooth paste is devoted to magic. But we are scientific too. Parbleu! We move with the times, we warlocks. Witch's Brew now complies with Pure Food and Drug Act. Familiars 100 per cent sterile. Sanitary brooms. Cellophane-wrapped curses. Father Satan in rubber gloves. Thanks to Lord Lister; or is it Pasteur? My idol."

The witch-pathologist gathered raw materials, consulted an ephemeris, ran off some calculations on an electronic computer and continued to chat.

"Fugit hora," Aquila said. "Your trouble, my old, is loss of sanity. Oui? Lost in one damn flight from reality and one damn desperate search for peace brought on by one unguarded look from me to you. Helas! I apologize for that, R.S.V.P." With what looked like a miniature tennis line-marker, he rolled a circle around Halsyon on the dais. "But your trouble is, to wit: You search for the peace of infancy. You should be fighting to acquire the peace of maturity, n'est-ce pas? Jeez." Aquila drew circles and pentagons with a glittering compass and rule, weighed out powders on a microbeam balance, dropped various liquids into crucibles from calibrated burettes, and continued: "Many warlocks do brisk trade in potions from Fountains of Youths. Oh yes. Are many youths and many fountains; but none for you. No. Youth is not for artists. Age is the cure. We must purge your youth and grow you up, nicht wahr?"

"No," Halsyon argued. "No. Youth is the art. Youth is the dream. Youth is the blessing."

"For some, yes. For many, not. Not for you. You are cursed, my adolescent. We must purge you. Lust for power. Lust for sex. Injustice collecting. Escape from reality. Passion for revenges. Oh yes, Father Freud is also my idol. We wipe your slate clean at very small price."

"What price?"

"You will see when we are finished."

Mr. Aquila deposited liquids and powders around the helpless artist in crucibles and petri dishes. He measured and cut fuses, set up a train from the circle to an electric timer which he carefully adjusted. He went to a shelf of serum bottles, took down a small Woulff vial numbered 5-271-009, filled a syringe and meticulously injected Halsyon.

"We begin," he said, "the purge of your dreams. Voilà."

He tripped the electric timer and stepped behind a lead shield. There was a moment of silence. Suddenly black music crashed from a concealed loudspeaker and a recorded voice began an intolerable chant. In quick succession the powders and liquids around Halsyon burst into flame. He was engulfed in music and fire. The world began to spin around him in a roaring confusion. . . .

*

The president of the United Nations came to him. He was tall and gaunt, sprightly but bitter. He was wringing his hands in dismay.

"Mr. Halsyon! Mr. Halsyon!" he cried. "Where you been, my cupcake? God damn. Hoc tempore. Do you know what has happened?"

"No," Halsyon answered. "What's happened?"

"After your escape from the looney bin. Bango! Atom bombs everywhere. The two-hour war. It is over. Hora fugit, old faithful, Virility is over."

"What!"

"Hard radiation, Mr. Halsyon, has destroyed the virility of the world. God damn. You are the only man left capable of engendering children. No doubt on account of a mysterious mutant strain in your makeup which it makes you different. Jeez."

"No."

"Oui. It is your responsibility to repopulate the world. We have taken for you a suite at the Odeon. It has three bedrooms. Three; my favorite. A prime number."

"Hot dog!" Halsyon said. "This is my big dream."

His progress to the Odeon was a triumph. He was garlanded with flowers, serenaded, hailed and cheered. Ecstatic women displayed themselves wickedly before him, begging for his attention. In his suite, Halsyon was wined and dined. A tall, gaunt man entered subserviently. He was sprightly but bitter. He had a list in his hand.

"I am World Procurer at your service, Mr. Halsyon," he said. He consulted his list. "God damn. Are 5,271,009 virgins clamoring for your attention. All guaranteed beautiful. Ewig-Weibliche. Pick a number from one to 5,000, 000."

"We'll start with a redhead," Halsyon said.

They brought him a redhead. She was slender and boyish, with a small hard bosom. The next was fuller with a rollicking rump. The fifth was Junoesque and her breasts were like African pears. The tenth was a voluptuous Rembrandt. The twentieth was wiry. The thirtieth was slender and boyish with a small hard bosom.

"Haven't we met before?" Halsyon inquired.

"No," she said.

The next was fuller with a rollicking rump.

"The body is familiar," Halsyon said.

"No," she answered.

The fiftieth was Junoesque with breasts like African pears.

"Surely?" Halsyon said.

"Never," she answered.

The World Procurer entered with Halsyon's morning aphrodisiac.

"Never touch the stuff," Halsyon said.

"God damn," the Procurer exclaimed. "You are a veritable giant. An elephant. No wonder you are the beloved Adam. Tant soit peu. No wonder they all weep for love of you." He drank off the aphrodisiac himself.

"Have you noticed they're all getting to look alike?" Halsyon complained.

"But no! Are all different. Parbleu! This is an insult to my office."

"Oh, they're different from one to another, but the types keep repeating."

"Ah? This is life, my old. All life is cyclic. Have you not, as an artist, noticed?"

"I didn't think it applied to love."

"To all things. Wahrheit und Dichtung."

"What was that you said about them weeping?"

"Oui. They all weep."

"Why?"

"For ecstatic love of you. God damn."

Halsyon thought over the succession of boyish, rollicking, Junoesque, Rembrandtesque, wiry, red, blonde, brunette, white, black and brown women.

"I hadn't noticed," he said.

"Observe today, my world father. Shall we commence?" It was true. Halsyon hadn't noticed. They all wept. He was flattered but depressed.

"Why don't you laugh a little?" he asked.

They would not or could not.

Upstairs on the Odeon roof where Halsyon took his afternoon exercise, he questioned his trainer who was a tall, gaunt man with a sprightly but bitter expression.

"Ah?" said the trainer. "God damn. I don't know, old Scotch and soda. Perhaps because it is a traumatic experience for them."

"Traumatic?" Halsyon puffed. "Why? What do I do to them?"

"Ah-ha? You joke, eh? All the world knows what you do to them."

"No, I mean . . . How can it be traumatic? They're all fighting to get to me, aren't they? Don't I come up to expectations?"

"A mystery. Tripotage. Now, beloved father of the world, we practice the push-ups. Ready? Begin."

Downstairs, in the Odeon restaurant, Halsyon questioned the head waiter, a tall, gaunt man with a sprightly manner but bitter expression.

"We are men of the world, Mr. Halsyon. Suo jure. Surely you understand. These women love you and can expect no more than one night of love. God damn. Naturally they are disappointed."

"What do they want?"

"What every woman wants, my gateway to the west. A permanent relationship. Marriage."

"Marriage!"

"Oui."

"All of them?"

"Oui."

"All right. I'll marry all 5,271,009."

But the World Procurer objected. "No, no, no, young Lochinvar. God damn. Impossible. Aside from religious difficulties there are human also. Who could manage such a harem?"

"Then I'll marry one."

"No, no, no. Pensez à moi. How could you make the choice? How could you select? By lottery, drawing straws, tossing coins?"

"I've already selected one."

"Ah? Which?"

"My girl," Halsyon said slowly. "Judith Field."

"So. Your sweetheart?"

"Yes."

"She is far down on the list of 5,000,000."

"She's always been number one on my list. I want Judith." Halsyon sighed. "I remember how she looked at the Beaux Arts Ball. . . . There was a full moon. . . ."

"But there will be no full moon until the twenty-sixth."

"I want Judith."

"The others will tear her apart out of jealousy. No, no, no, Mr. Halsyon, we must stick to the schedule. One night for all, no more for any."

"I want Judith . . . or else."

"It will have to be discussed in council. God damn."

It was discussed in the U. N. council by a dozen delegates, all tall, gaunt, sprightly but bitter. It was decided to permit Jeffrey Halsyon one secret marriage.

"But no domestic ties," the World Procurer warned. "No faithfulness to your wife. That must be understood. We cannot spare you from our program. You are indispensable."

They brought the lucky Judith Field to the Odeon. She was a tall, dark girl with cropped curly hair and lovely tennis legs. Halsyon took her hand. The World Procurer tip-toed out.

"Hello, darling," Halsyon murmured.

Judith looked at him with loathing. Her eyes were wet, her face was bruised from weeping.

"Hello, darling," Halsyon repeated.

"If you touch me, Jeff," Judith said in a strangled voice, "I'll kill you."

"Judy!"

"That disgusting man explained everything to me. He didn't seem to understand when I tried to explain to him. . . . I was praying you'd be dead before it was my turn."

"But this is marriage, Judy."

"I'd rather die than be married to you."

"I don't believe you. We've been in love for—"

"For God's sake, Jeff, love's over for you. Don't you understand? Those women cry because they hate you. I hate you. The world loathes you. You're disgusting."

Halsyon stared at the girl and saw the truth in her face. In an excess of rage he tried to seize her. She fought him bitterly. They careened around the huge living room of the suite, overturning furniture, their breath hissing, their fury mounting. Halsyon struck Judith Field with his big fist to end the struggle once and for all. She reeled back, clutched at a drape, smashed through a french window and fell fourteen floors to the street like a gyrating doll.

Halsyon looked down in horror. A crowd gathered around the smashed body. Faces upturned. Fists shook. An ominous growl began. The World Procurer dashed into the suite.

"My old! My blue!" he cried. "What have you done? Per conto. It is a spark that will ignite savagery. You are in very grave danger. God damn."

"Is it true they all hate me?"

"Hélas, then you have discovered the truth? That indiscreet girl. I warned her. Oui. You are loathed."

"But you told me I was loved. The new Adam. Father of the new world."

"Oui. You are the father, but what child does not hate its father? You are also a legal rapist. What woman does not hate being forced to embrace a man . . . even by necessity for survival? Come quickly, my rock and rye. Passim. You are in great danger."

He dragged Halsyon to a back elevator and took him down to the Odeon cellar.

"The army will get you out. We take you to Turkey at once and effect a compromise."

Halsyon was transferred to the custody of a tall, gaunt, bitter army colonel who rushed him through underground passages to a side street, where a staff car was waiting. The colonel thrust Halsyon inside.

"Jacta alea est," he said to the driver. "Speed, my corporal. Protect old faithful. To the airport. Alors!"

"God damn, sir," the corporal replied. He saluted and started the car. As it twisted through the streets at breakneck speed, Halsyon glanced at him. He was a tall, gaunt man, sprightly but bitter.

"Kulturkampf der Menscheit," the corporal muttered. "Jeez!"

A giant barricade had been built across the street, improvised of ash barrels, furniture, overturned cars, traffic stanchions. The corporal was forced to brake the car. As he slowed for a U-turn, a mob of women appeared from doorways, cellars, stores. They were screaming. Some of them brandished improvised clubs.

"Excelsior!" the corporal cried. "God damn." He tried to pull his service gun out of its holster. The women yanked open the car doors and tore Halsyon and the corporal out. Halsyon broke free, struggled through the wild clubbing mob, dashed to the sidewalk, stumbled and dropped with a sickening yaw through an open coal chute. He shot down and spilled out into an endless black space. His head whirled. A stream of stars sailed before his eyes. . . .

*

And he drifted alone in space, a martyr, misunderstood, a victim of cruel injustice.

He was still chained to what had once been the wall of Cell 5, Block 27, Tier 100, Wing 9 of the Callisto Penitentiary until that unexpected gamma explosion had torn the vast fortress dungeon—Vaster than the Chateau d' If—apart. That explosion, he realized, had been detonated by the Grssh.

His assets were his convict clothes, a helmet, one cylinder of O2, his grim fury at the injustice that had been done him, and his knowledge of the secret of how the Grssh could be defeated in their maniacal quest for solar domination.

The Grssh, ghastly marauders from Omicron Ceti, space-degenerates, space-imperialists, cold-blooded, roach-like, depending for their food upon the psychotic horrors which they engendered in man through mental control and upon which they fed, were rapidly conquering the galaxy. There were irresistible, for they possessed the power of simul-kinesis—the ability to be in two places at the same time.

Against the vault of space, a dot of light moved, slowly, like a stricken meteor. It was a rescue ship, Halsyon realized, combing space for survivors of the explosion. He wondered whether the light of Jupiter, flooding him with rusty radiation, would make him visible to the rescuers. He wondered whether he wanted to be rescued at all.

"It will be the same thing again," Halsyon grated. "Falsely accused by Balorsen's robot. . . . Falsely convicted by Judith's father. . . . Repudiated by Judith herself. . . . Jailed again . . . and finally destroyed by the Grssh as they destroy the last strongholds of Terra. Why not die now?"

But even as he spoke he realized he lied. He was the one man with the one secret that could save the earth and the very galaxy itself. He must survive. He must fight.

With indomitable will, Halsyon struggled to his feet, fighting the constricting chains. With the steely strength he had developed as a penal laborer in the Grssh mines, he waved and shouted. The spot of light did not alter its slow course away from him. Then he saw the metal link of one of his chains strike a brilliant spark from the flinty rock. He resolved on a desperate expedient to signal the rescue ship.

He detached the plasti-hose of the O2 tank from his plasti-helmet, and permitted the stream of life-giving oxygen to spurt into space. With trembling hands, he gathered the links of his leg chain and dashed them against the rock under the oxygen. A spark glowed. The oxygen caught fire. A brilliant geyser of white flame spurted for half a mile into space.

Husbanding the last oxygen in his plasti-helmet, Halsyon twisted the cylinder slowly, sweeping the fan of flame back and forth in a last

desperate bid for rescue. The atmosphere in his plasti-helmet grew foul
and acrid. His ears roared. His sight flickered. At last his senses failed. .
. .

When he recovered consciousness he was in a plasti-cot in the cabin of
a starship. The high frequency whine told him they were in overdrive. He
opened his eyes. Balorsen stood before the plasti-cot, and Balorsen's
robot and High Judge Field, and his daughter Judith. Judith was weeping.
The robot was in magnetic plasti-clamps and winced as General Balorsen
lashed him again and again with a nuclear, plasti-whip.

"Parbleu! God damn!" the robot grated. "It is true I framed Jeff
Halsyon. Ouch! Flux de bouche. I was the space-pirate who space-
hijacked the space-freighter. God damn. Ouch! The space-bartender in
the Spaceman's Saloon was my accomplice. When Jackson wrecked the
space-cab I went to the space-garage and X-beamed the sonic *before*
Tantial murdered O'Leary. Aux armes. Jeez. Ouch!"

"There you have the confession, Halsyon," General Balorsen grated.
He was tall, gaunt, bitter. "By God. Ars est celare artem. You are
innocent."

"I falsely condemned you, old faithful," Judge Field grated. He was tall,
gaunt, bitter. "Can you forgive this God damn fool? We apologize."

"We wronged you, Jeff," Judith whispered. "How can you ever forgive
us? Say you forgive us."

"You're sorry for the way you treated me," Halsyon grated. "But it's
only because on account of a mysterious mutant strain in my makeup
which it makes me different, I'm the one man with the one secret that can
save the galaxy from the Grssh."

"No, no, no, old gin and tonic," General Balorsen pleaded. "God damn.
Don't hold grudges. Save us from the Grssh."

"Save us, faute de mieux, save us, Jeff," Judge Field put in. "Oh please,
Jeff, please," Judith whispered. "The Grssh are everywhere and coming
closer. We're taking you to the U. N. You must tell the council how to
stop the Grssh from being in two places at the same time." The starship
came out of overdrive and landed on Governor's Island where a
delegation of world dignitaries met the ship and rushed Halsyon to the
General Assembly room of the U. N. They drove down the strangely

rounded streets lined with strangely rounded buildings which had all been altered when it was discovered that the Grssh always appeared in comers. There was not a comer or an angle left on all Terra.

The General Assembly was filled when Halsyon entered. Hundreds of tall, gaunt, bitter diplomats applauded as he made his way to the podium, still dressed in convict plasti-clothes. Halsyon looked around resentfully.

"Yes," he grated. "You all applaud. You all revere me now; but where were you when I was framed, convicted and jailed . . . an innocent man? Where were you then?"

"Halsyon, forgive us. God damn!" they shouted.

"I will not forgive you, I suffered for seventeen years in the Grssh mines. Now it's your turn to suffer."

"Please, Halsyon!"

"Where are your experts? Your professors? Your specialists? Where are your electronic calculators? Your super thinking machines? Let them solve the mystery of the Grssh."

"They can't, old whiskey and soda. Entre nous. They're stopped cold. Save us, Halsyon. Auf wiedersehen."

Judith took his arm. "Not for my sake, Jeff," she whispered. "I know you'll never forgive me for the injustice I did you. But for the sake of all the other girls in the galaxy who love and are loved."

"I still love you, Judy."

"I've always loved you, Jeff."

"Okay. I didn't want to tell them but you talked me into it." Halsyon raised his hand for silence. In the ensuing hush he spoke softly. "The secret is this, gentlemen. Your calculators have assembled data to ferret out the secret weakness of the Grssh. They have not been able to find any. consequently you have assumed that the Grssh have no secret weakness. *That was a wrong assumption.*"

The General Assembly held its breath.

"Here is the secret. *You should have assumed there was something wrong with the calculators.*"

"God damn!" the General Assembly cried. "Why didn't we think of that? God damn!"

"*And I know what's wrong!*"

There was a deathlike hush.

The door of the General Assembly burst open. Professor Deathhush, tall, gaunt, bitter, tottered in. "Eureka!" he cried. "I've found it. God damn. Something wrong with the thinking machines. Three comes *after* two, not before." The General Assembly broke into cheers. Professor Deathhush was seized and pummeled happily. Bottles were opened. His health was drunk. Several medals were pinned on him. He beamed.

"Hey!" Halsyon called. "That was my secret. I'm the one man who on account of a mysterious mutant strain in my—"

The ticker-tape began pounding: ATTENTION. ATTENTION. HUSHENKOV IN MOSCOW REPORTS DEFECT IN CALCULATORS. 3 COMES AFTER 2 AND NOT BEFORE, REPEAT: AFTER (UNDERSCORE) NOT BEFORE.

A postman ran in. "Special delivery from Doctor Lifehush at Caltech. Says something's wrong with the thinking machines. Three comes after two, not before."

A telegraph boy delivered a wire: THINKING MACHINE WRONG STOP TWO COMES BEFORE THREE STOP NOT AFTER STOP. VON DREAMHUSH, HEIDELBERG.

A bottle was thrown through the window. It crashed on the floor revealing a bit of paper on which was scrawled: *Did you ever stopp to thinc that maibe the nomber 3 comes after 2 insted of in front? Down with the Grish. Mr. Hush-Hush.*

Halsyon buttonholed Judge Field. "What the hell is this?" he demanded. "I thought I was the one man in the world with that secret."

"HimmelHerrGott! " Judge Field replied impatiently. "You are all alike. You dream you are the one men with a secret, the one men with a wrong, the one men with an injustice, with a girl, without a girl, with or without anything. God damn. You bore me, you one-man dreamers. Get lost."

Judge Field shouldered him aside. General Balorsen shoved him back. Judith Field ignored him. Balorsen's robot sneakily tripped him into a comer of the crowd where a Grssh, also in a crowded comer on Neptune, appeared, did something unspeakable to Halsyon and disappeared with him, screaming, jerking and sobbing into a horror that was a delicious meal for the Grssh but a plasti-nightmare for Halsyon . . .

From which his mother awakened him and said, "This'll teach you not to sneak peanut-butter sandwiches in the middle of the night. Jeffrey."

"Mama?"

"Yes. It's time to get up, dear. You'll be late for school."

She left the room. He looked around. He looked at himself. It was true. True! The glorious realization came upon him. His dream had come true. He was ten years old again, in the flesh that was his ten-year-old body, in the home that was his boyhood home, in the life that had been his life in the nineteen thirties. And within his head was the knowledge, the experience, the sophistication of a man of thirty-three.

"Oh joy!" he cried. "It'll be a triumph. A triumph!"

He would be the school genius. He would astonish his parents, amaze his teachers, confound the experts. He would win scholarships. He would settle the hash of that kid Rennahan who used to bully him. He would hire a typewriter and write all the successful plays and stories and novels he remembered. He would cash in on that lost opportunity with Judy Field behind the memorial in Isham Park. He would steal inventions and discoveries, get in on the ground floor of new industries, make bets, play the stock-market. He would own the world by the time he caught up with himself.

He dressed with difficulty. He had forgotten where his clothes were kept. He ate breakfast with difficulty. This was no time to explain to his mother that he'd gotten into the habit of starting the day with Irish coffee. He missed his morning cigarette. He had no idea where his school-books were. His mother had trouble starting him out.

"Jeff's in one of his moods," he heard her mutter. "I hope he gets through the day."

The day started with Rennahan ambushing him at the Boy's Entrance. Halsyon remembered him as a big tough kid with a vicious expression. He was astonished to discover that Rennahan was skinny and harassed, and obviously compelled by some bedevilments to be omnivorously aggressive.

"Why, you're not hostile to me," Halsyon exclaimed. "You're just a mixed-up kid who's trying to prove something."

Rennahan punched him.

"Look, kid," Halsyon said kindly. "You really want to be friends with the world. You're just insecure. That's why you're compelled to fight."

Rennahan was deaf to spot analysis. He punched Halsyon harder. It hurt.

"Oh leave me alone," Halsyon said. "Go prove yourself on somebody else."

Rennahan, with two swift motions, knocked Halsyon's books from under his arm and ripped his fly open. There was nothing for it but to fight. Twenty years of watching films of the future Joe Louis did nothing for Halsyon. He was thoroughly licked. He was also late for school. Now was his chance to amaze his teachers.

"The fact is," he explained to Miss Ralph of the fifth grade. "I had a run-in with a neurotic. I can speak for his left hook but I won't answer for his compulsions." Miss Ralph slapped him and sent him to the principal with a note, reporting unheard-of insolence.

"The only thing unheard of in this school," Halsyon told Mr. Snider, "is psychoanalysis. How can you pretend to be competent teachers if you don't—"

"Dirty little boy!" Mr. Snider interrupted angrily. He was tall, gaunt, bitter. "So you've been reading dirty books, eh?"

"What the hell's dirty about Freud?"

"And using profane language, eh? You need a lesson, you filthy little animal."

He was sent home with a note requesting an immediate consultation with his parents regarding the withdrawal of Jeffrey Halsyon from school as a degenerate in desperate need of correction and vocational guidance.

Instead of going home he went to a newsstand to check the papers for events on which to get a bet down. The headlines were full of the pennant race. But who the hell won the pennant in 1931? And the series? He couldn't for the life of him remember. And the stock market? He couldn't remember anything about that either. He'd never been particularly interested in such matters as a boy. There was nothing planted in his memory to call upon.

He tried to get into the library for further checks. The librarian, tall, gaunt, and bitter, would not permit him to enter until children's hour in the afternoon. He loafed on the streets. Wherever he loafed he was chased by gaunt and bitter adults. He was beginning to realize that ten-year-old boys had limited opportunities to amaze the world.

At lunch hour he met Judy Field and accompanied her home from school. He was appalled by her knobby knees and black corkscrew curls. He didn't like the way she smelled either. But he was rather taken with her mother who was the image of the Judy he remembered. He forgot himself with Mrs. Field and did one or two things that indeed confounded her. She drove him out of the house and then telephoned his mother, her voice shaking with indignation.

Halsyon went down to the Hudson River and hung around the ferry docks until he was chased. He went to a stationery store to inquire about typewriter rentals and was chased. He searched for a quiet place to sit, think, plan, perhaps begin the recall of a successful story. There was no quiet place to which a small boy would be admitted.

He slipped into his house at 4:30, dropped his books in his room, stole into the living room, sneaked a cigarette and was on his way out when he discovered his mother and father inspecting him. His mother looked shocked. His father was gaunt and bitter.

"Oh," Halsyon said. "I suppose Snider phoned. I'd forgotten about that."

"*Mister Snider*," his mother said.

"And Mrs. Field," his father said.

"Look," Halsyon began. "We'd better get this straightened out. Will you listen to me for a few minutes? I have something startling to tell you and we've got to plan what to do about it. I—"

He yelped. His father had taken him by the ear and was marching him down the hall. Parents did not listen to children for a few minutes. They did not listen at all.

"Pop . . . Just a minute . . . Please! I'm trying to explain. I'm not really ten years old. I'm thirty-three. There's been a freak in time, see? On account of a mysterious mutant strain in my makeup which—"

"Damn you! Be quiet!" his father shouted. The pain of his big hands, the suppressed fury in his voice silenced Halsyon. He suffered himself to be led out of the house, down four blocks to the school, and up one flight to Mr. Snider's office where a public school psychologist was waiting with the principal. He was a tall man, gaunt, bitter, but sprightly.

"Ah yes, yes," he said. "So this is our little degenerate. Our Scarface Al Capone, eh? Come, we take him to the clinic and there I shall take his journal in time. We will hope for the best. Nisi prius. He cannot be all bad." He took Halsyon's arm. Halsyon pulled his arm away and said, "Listen, you're an adult, intelligent man. You'll listen to me. My father's got emotional problems that blind him to the—"

His father gave him a tremendous box on the ear, grabbed his arm and thrust it back into the psychologist's grasp. Halsyon burst into tears. The psychologist led him out of the office and into the tiny school infirmary. Halsyon was hysterical. He was trembling with frustration and terror.

"Won't anybody listen to me?" he sobbed. "Won't anybody try to understand? Is this what we're all like to kids? Is this what all kids go through?"

"Gently, my sausage," the psychologist murmured. He popped a pill into Halsyon's mouth and forced him to drink some water.

"You're all so damned inhuman," Halsyon wept. "You keep us out of your world, but you keep barging into ours. If you don't respect us why don't you leave us alone?"

"You begin to understand, eh?" the psychologist said. "We are two different breeds of animal, childrens and adults. God damn. I speak to you with frankness. Les absents ont toujours tort. There is no meetings of the minds. Jeez. There is nothing but war. It is why all childrens grow up hating their childhoods and searching for revenges. But there is never revenges. Pari mutuel. How can there be? Can a cat insult a king?"

"It's . . . S'hateful," Halsyon mumbled. The pill was taking effect rapidly. "Whole world's hateful. Full of conflicts'n'insults 'at can't be r'solved . . . or paid back. . . . S'like a joke somebody's playin' on us. Silly joke without point. Isn't?"

As he slid down into darkness, he could hear the psychologist chuckle, but couldn't for the life of him understand what he was laughing at. . . .

*

He picked up his spade and followed the first clown into the cemetery. The first clown was a tall man, gaunt, bitter, but sprightly.

"Is she to be buried in Christian burial that willfully seeks her own salvation?" the first clown asked.

"I tell thee she is," Halsyon answered. "And therefore make her grave straight: the crowner hath sat on her, and finds it Christian burial."

"How can that be, unless she drowned herself in her own defense?"

"Why, 'tis found so."

They began to dig the grave. The first clown thought the matter over, then said, "It must be *se offendendo*; it cannot be else. For here lies the point: if I drown myself wittingly, it argues an act: and an act hath three branches; it is, to act, to do, to perform: argal, she drowned herself wittingly."

"Nay, but hear you, goodman delver—" Halsyon began.

"Give me leave," the first clown interrupted and went on with a tiresome discourse on quest-law. Then he turned sprightly and cracked a few professional jokes. At last Halsyon got away and went down to Yaughan's for a drink. When he returned, the first clown was cracking jokes with a couple of gentlemen who had wandered into the graveyard. One of them made quite a fuss about a skull.

The burial procession arrived; the coffin, the dead girl's brother, the king and queen, the priests and lords. They buried her, and the brother and one of the gentlemen began to quarrel over her grave. Halsyon paid no attention. There was a pretty girl in the procession, dark, with cropped curly hair and lovely long legs. He winked at her. She winked back. Halsyon edged over toward her, speaking with his eyes and she answered him saucily the same way.

Then he picked up his spade and followed the first clown into the cemetery. The first clown was a tall man, gaunt, with a bitter expression but a sprightly manner.

"Is she to be buried in Christian burial that wilfully seeks her own salvation?" the first clown asked.

"I tell thee she is," Halsyon answered. "And therefore make her grave straight: the crowner hath sat on her, and finds it Christian burial."

"How can that be, unless she drowned herself in her own defense?"

"Didn't you ask me that before?" Halsyon inquired. "Shut up, old faithful. Answer the question."

"I could swear this happened before."

"God damn. Will you answer? Jeez."

"Why, 'tis found so."

They began to dig the grave. The first clown thought the matter over and began a long discourse on quest-law. After that he turned sprightly and cracked trade jokes. At last Halsyon got away and went down to Yaughan's for a drink. When he returned there were a couple of strangers at the grave and then the burial procession arrived.

There was a pretty girl in the procession, dark, with cropped curly hair and lovely long legs. Halsyon winked at her. She winked back. Halsyon edged over toward her, speaking with his eyes and she answering him the same way.

"What's your name?" he whispered.

"Judith," she answered.

"I have your name tattooed on me, Judith."

"You're lying, sir."

"I can prove it, Madam. I'll show you where I was tattooed."

"And where is that?"

"In Yaughan's tavern. It was done by a sailor off the Golden Hind. Will you see it with me tonight?"

Before she could answer, he picked up his spade and followed the first clown into the cemetery. The first clown was a tall man, gaunt, with a bitter expression but a sprightly manner.

"For God's sake!" Halsyon complained. "I could swear this happened before."

"Is she to be buried in Christian burial that willfully seeks her own salvation?" the first clown asked.

"I just know we've been through all this."

"Will you answer the question!"

"Listen," Halsyon said doggedly. "Maybe I'm crazy; maybe not. But I've got a spooky feeling that all this happened before. It seems unreal. Life seems unreal."

The first clown shook his head. "HimmelHerrGott," he muttered. "It is as I feared. Lux et veritas. On account of a mysterious mutant strain in your makeup which it makes you different, you are treading on thin water. Ewigkeit! Answer the question."

"If I've answered it once, I've answered it a hundred times."

"Old ham and eggs," the first clown burst out, "you have answered it 5,271,009 times. God damn. Answer again."

"Why?"

"Because you must. Pot au feu. It is the life we must live."

"You call this life? Doing the same things over and over again? Saying the same things? Winking at girls and never getting any further?"

"No, no, no, my Donner and Blitzen. Do not question. It is a conspiracy we dare not fight. This is the life every man lives. Every man does the same things over and over. There is no escape."

"Why is there no escape?"

"I dare not say; I dare not. Vox populi. Others have questioned and disappeared. It is a conspiracy. I'm afraid."

"Afraid of what?"

"Of our owners."

"What? We are owned?"

"Si. Ach, ja! All of us, young mutant. There is no reality. There is no life, no freedom, no will. God damn. Don't you realize? We are . . . We are all characters in a book. As the book is read, we dance our dances; when the book is read again, we dance again. E pluribus unum. Is she to be buried in Christian burial that willfully seeks her own salvation?"

"What are you saying?" Halsyon cried in horror. "We're puppets?"

"Answer the question."

"If there's no freedom, no free will, how can we be talking like this?"

"Whoever's reading our book is day-dreaming, my capital of Dakota. Idem est. Answer the question."

"I will not. I'm going to revolt. I'll dance for our owners no longer. I'll find a better life. . . . . I'll find reality."

"No, no! It's madness, Jeffrey! Cul-de-sac!"

"All we need is one brave leader. The rest will follow. We'll smash the conspiracy that chains us!"

"It cannot be done. Play it safe. Answer the question." Halsyon answered the question by picking up his spade and bashing in the head of the first clown who appeared not to notice. "Is she to be buried in Christian burial that willfully seeks her own salvation?" he asked.

"Revolt!" Halsyon cried and bashed him again. The clown started to sing. The two gentlemen appeared. One said: "Has this fellow no feeling of business that he sings at grave-making?"

"Revolt! Follow me!" Halsyon shouted and swung his spade against the gentlemen's melancholy head. He paid no attention. He chatted with his friend and the first clown. Halsyon whirled like a dervish, laying about him with his spade. The gentleman picked up a skull and philosophized over some person or persons named Yorick.

The funeral procession approached. Halsyon attacked it, whirling and turning, around and around with the clotted frenzy of a man in a dream.

"Stop reading the book," he shouted. "Let me out of the pages. Can you hear me? Stop reading the book! I'd rather be in a world of my own making. Let me go!" There was a mighty clap of thunder, as of the covers of a mighty book slamming shut. In an instant Halsyon was swept spinning into the third compartment of the seventh circle of the Inferno in the fourteenth Canto of the Divine Comedy where they who have sinned against art are tormented by flakes of fire which are eternally showered down upon them. There he shrieked until he had provided sufficient amusement. Only then was he permitted to devise a text of his own . . . and he formed a new world, a romantic world, a world of his fondest

dreams. . . .

*

He was the last man on earth.

He was the last man on earth and he howled.

The hills, the valleys, the mountains and streams were his, his alone, and he howled.

Five million two hundred and seventy-one thousand and nine houses were his for shelter, 5,271,009 beds were his for sleeping. The shops were his for the breaking and entering. The jewels of the world were his; the toys, the tools, the playthings, the necessities, the luxuries . . . all belonged to the last man on earth, and he howled.

He left the country mansion in the fields of Connecticut where he had taken up residence; he crossed into Westchester, howling; he ran south along what had once been the Hendrick Hudson Highway, howling; he crossed the bridge into Manhattan, howling; he ran downtown past lonely skyscrapers, department stores, amusement palaces, howling. He howled down Fifth Avenue, and at the comer of Fiftieth Street he saw a human being.

She was alive, breathing; a beautiful woman. She was tall and dark with cropped curly hair and lovely long legs. She wore a white blouse, tiger-skin riding breeches and patent leather boots. She carried a rifle. She wore a revolver on her hip. She was eating stewed tomatoes from a can and she stared at Halsyon in unbelief. He ran up to her.

"I thought I was the last human on earth," she said.

"You're the last woman," Halsyon howled. "I'm the last man. Are you a dentist?"

"No," she said. "I'm the daughter of the unfortunate Professor Field whose well-intentioned but ill-advised experiment in nuclear fission has wiped mankind off the face of the earth with the exception of you and me who, no doubt on account of some mysterious mutant strain in our makeup which it makes us different, are the last of the old civilization and the first of the new."

"Didn't your father teach you anything about dentistry?"

"No," she said.

"Then lend me your gun for a minute."

She unholstered the revolver and handed it to Halsyon, meanwhile keeping her rifle ready. Halsyon cocked the gun.

"I wish you'd been a dentist," he said.

"I'm a beautiful woman with an I.Q. of 141 which is more important for the propagation of a brave new beautiful race of men to inherit the good green earth," she said.

"Not with my teeth it isn't," Halsyon howled.

He clapped the revolver to his temple and blew his brains out.

*

He awoke with a splitting headache. He was lying on the tile dais alongside the stool, his bruised temple pressed against the cold floor. Mr.

Aquila had emerged from the lead shield and was turning on an exhaust fan to clear the air.

"Bravo, my liver and onions," he chuckled. "The last one you did by yourself, eh? No assistance from yours truly required. Meglio tarde che mai. But you went over with a crack before I could catch you. God damn."

He helped Halsyon to his feet and led him into the consultation room where he seated him on a velvet chaise longue and gave him a glass of brandy.

"Guaranteed free of drugs," he said. "Noblesse oblige. Only the best spiritus frumenti. Now we discuss what we have done, eh? Jeez."

He sat down behind the desk, still sprightly, still bitter, and regarded Halsyon with kindliness. "Man lives by his decisions, n'est-ce pas?" he began. "We agree, oui? A man has some five million two hundred seventy-one thousand and nine decisions to make in the course of his life. Peste! It is a prime number? N'importe. Do you agree?"

Halsyon nodded.

"So, my coffee and doughnuts, it is the maturity of these decisions that decides whether a man is a man or a child. Nicht wahr? Malgré nous. A man cannot start making adult decisions until he has purged himself of the dreams of childhood. God damn. Such fantasies. They must go."

"No," Halsyon said slowly. "It's the dreams that make my art . . . the dreams and fantasies that I translate into line and color. . ."

"God damn! Yes. Agreed. Maître d'hôtel: But adult dreams, not baby dreams. Baby dreams. Pfui! All men have them. . . . To be the last man on earth and own the earth . . . To be the last fertile man on earth and own the women . . . To go back in time with the advantage of adult knowledge and win victories . . . To escape reality with the dream that life is make-believe . . . To escape responsibility with a fantasy of heroic injustice, of martyrdom with a happy ending . . . And there are hundreds more, equally popular, equally empty. God bless Father Freud and his merry men. He applies the quietus to such nonsense. Sic semper tyrannis. Avaunt!"

"But if everybody has those dreams, they can't be bad, can they?"

"God damn. Everybody in fourteenth century had lice. Did that make it good? No, my young, such dreams are for childrens. Too many adults are still childrens. It is you, the artists, who must lead them out as I have led you. I purge you; now you purge them."

"Why did you do this?"

"Because I have faith in you. Sic vos non vobis. It will not be easy for you. A long hard road and lonely."

"I suppose I ought to feel grateful," Halsyon muttered, "but I feel . . . well . . . empty. Cheated."

"Oh yes, God damn. If you live with one Jeez big ulcer long enough you miss him when he's cut out. You were hiding in an ulcer. I have robbed you of said refuge. Ergo: you feel cheated. Wait! You will feel even more cheated. There was a price to pay, I told you. You have paid it. Look."

Mr. Aquila held up a hand mirror. Halsyon glanced into it, then started and stared. A fifty-year-old face stared back at him: lined, hardened, solid, determined. Halsyon leaped to his feet.

"Gently, gently," Mr. Aquila admonished. "It is not so bad. It is damned good. You are still thirty-three in age of physique. You have lost none of your life . . . only all of your youth. What have you lost? A pretty face to lure young girls? Is that why you are wild?"

"Christ!" Halsyon cried.

"All right. Still gently, my child. Here you are, purged, disillusioned, unhappy, bewildered, one foot on the hard road to maturity. Would you like this to have happened or not have happened? Si. I can do. This can never have happened. Spurlos versenkt. It is ten seconds from your escape. You can have your pretty young face back. You can be recaptured. You can return to the safe ulcer of the womb . . . a child again. Would you like same?"

"You can't."

"Sauve qui peut, my Pike's Peak. I can. There is no end to the 15,000 angstrom band."

"Damn you! Are you Satan? Lucifer? Only the devil could have such powers."

"Or angels, my old."

"You don't look like an angel. You look like Satan."

"Ah? Ha? But Satan was an angel before he fell. He has many relations on high. Surely there are family resemblances. God damn." Mr. Aquila stopped laughing. He leaned across the desk and the sprightliness was gone from his face. Only the bitterness remained. "Shall I tell you who I am, my chicken? Shall I explain why one unguarded look from this phizz toppled you over the brink?" Halsyon nodded, unable to speak.

"I am a scoundrel, a black sheep, a scapegrace, a blackguard. I am a remittance man. Yes. God damn! I am a remittance man." Mr. Aquila's eyes turned into wounds. "By your standards I am the great man of infinite power and variety. So was the remittance man from Europe to naive natives on the beaches of Tahiti. Eh? And so am I to you as I comb the beaches of the stars for a little amusement, a little hope, a little joy to while away the lonely years of my exile. . . .

"I am bad," Mr. Aquila said in a voice of chilling desperation. "I am rotten. There is no place in my home that can tolerate me. They pay me to stay away. And there are moments, unguarded, when my sickness and my despair fill my eyes and strike terror into your innocent souls. As I strike terror into you now. Yes?"

Halsyon nodded again.

"Be guided by me. It was the child in Solon Aquila that destroyed him and led him into the sickness that destroyed his life. Oui. I too suffer from baby fantasies from which I cannot escape. Do not make the same mistake. I beg of you . . ." Mr. Aquila glanced at his wrist-watch and leaped up. The sprightly returned to his manner. "Jeez. It's late. Time to make up your mind, old bourbon and soda. Which will it be? Old face or pretty face? The reality of dreams or the dream of reality?"

"How many decisions did you say we have to make in a lifetime?"

"Five million two hundred and seventy-one thousand and nine. Give or take a thousand. God damn."

"And which one is this for me?"

"Ah? Vérité sans peur. The two million six hundred and thirty-five thousand five hundred and fourth . . . off hand."

"But it's the big one."

"They are all big." Mr. Aquila stepped to the door, placed his hand on the buttons of a rather complicated switch and cocked an eye at Halsyon.

"Voila tout," he said. "It rests with you."

"I'll take it the hard way," Halsyon decided.

There was a silver chime from the switch, a fizzing aura, a soundless explosion, and Jeffrey Halsyon was ready for his 2,635,505th decision.

Lightning Source UK Ltd.
Milton Keynes UK
UKOW04f2233251115

263547UK00005B/424/P